James Stevenson

THE
OLDEST ELF

A Mulberry Paperback Book • New York

For Ellen and Pam

Watercolor paints and a black pen were used for the full-color art.
The text type is Veljovic Medium.

Inquiries should be addressed to Greenwillow Books, a division of William Morrow & Company, Inc., 1350 Avenue of the Americas, New York, New York 10019.
www.williammorrow.com
Printed in the United States of America

The Library of Congress has cataloged the Greenwillow Books edition of *The Oldest Elf* as follows:
Stevenson, James (date)
The oldest elf / by James Stevenson.
    p. cm.

Summary: Elwyn, Santa's oldest elf, and Blitzen, a retired reindeer, help Santa out for one last Christmas.
ISBN 0-688-13755-5 (trade).
ISBN 0-688-13756-3 (lib. bdg.)
[1. Christmas—Fiction. 2. Santa Claus—Fiction.]
I. Title. PZ7.S84748Oj 1996 [E]—dc20
94-25355 CIP AC

10 9 8 7 6 5 4 3 2 1
First Mulberry Edition, 1998
ISBN 0-688-16154-5

It was almost Christmas.
All night long Santa's workshop buzzed and hummed
and screeched. Colored lights flashed on and off.

In the stable the reindeer had a hard time
trying to sleep.

"All those lights and noises," said Prancer.

"I can't get any rest at all."

"How soon is Christmas Eve?" asked Donner.

"Tomorrow night," said Dancer.

"Thank goodness," said Prancer.

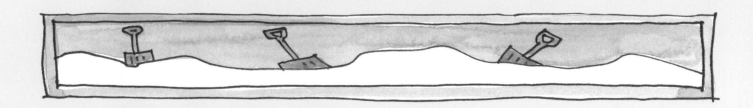

In the workshop the elves were building
video games that beeped, helicopters that
whined, dolls that walked and talked,
fire engines that wailed, racing cars that
went wherever they were told to go.
"Anybody need more batteries?" said
Santa Claus.

The only quiet place was a room in the
cellar, where nobody ever went.
It was the room where Elwyn, the oldest
elf, made toys.
In Elwyn's room the sounds were soft—
sandpaper smoothing the deck of a wooden
boat, or a brush painting a piggy bank.
Sometimes it was Elwyn himself, humming
a tune from long ago.

"It must be getting close to Christmas,"
said Elwyn, "and I still have lots to do."
He searched for a calendar.
At last he found one, but it said 1984.

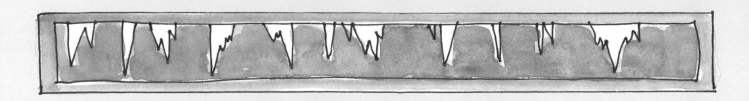

He went up the stairs to the workshop.
"What day is this?" he called to one of the
  younger elves.
"The day before Christmas Eve, Elwyn,"
  said one elf.
"That late?" said Elwyn.

He put the wheels
on a pedal car.

He tied a ribbon
on a China doll.

He painted a set
of blocks.

He squirted oil into
the wind-up toys and
made sure each one
had a key that worked.

He fixed the strings
on a wooden puppet.

He tuned
a small guitar.

He brushed the mane
and tail of a rocking horse.

He polished
the brass buttons
on a toy soldier.

He wound a toy cuckoo clock and
set the hands for just before the hour.
A minute later a bird popped out
and said, "Cuckoo!"

When Elwyn was all finished, he put
the toys in a sack and dragged it slowly
up the stairs.

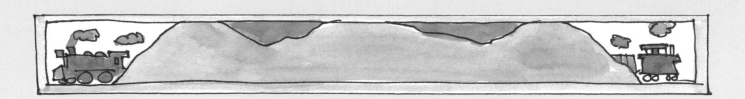

The workshop was silent and deserted.

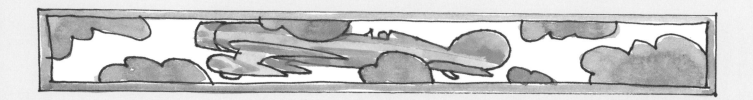

Elwyn put on his coat and hat. He pulled his sack
outdoors and over to the stable.
He saw hoofprints and the two tracks of Santa's sleigh.
The tracks went a short distance. Then there was just
plain snow.

"You missed them," said an old voice.
"They left twenty minutes ago."
"Who's that?" said Elwyn.
"It's me, Blitzen," said Blitzen.
"Hello, Blitzen," said Elwyn. "Did you miss
  them, too?"
"Heck, no," said Blitzen. "I got too old for
  those last-minute rides through the night.
  No more 'On, Donner! On, Blitzen!' for me."

"What do they do without you?" asked
  Elwyn.
"Santa found a doe named Josephine," said
  Blitzen. "Now I stay home in the warm
  straw."
"I guess you deserve a rest," said Elwyn.
"What's in the sack?" said Blitzen.
"Toys," said Elwyn. "I made them myself."
"It's a shame you missed the sleigh," said
  Blitzen. "All that work for nothing."
"This is a very sad Christmas," said Elwyn.
"And it's all my fault." He began to walk
  away. "Good night, Blitzen," he said.
"Good night, Elwyn," said Blitzen.

Then he saw that Elwyn had left his sack.
"You forgot your toys!" he called.
But the wind was strong, and Elwyn was
too far away to hear.

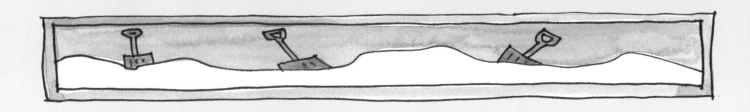

Snow began to fall harder. Soon the
toys were half buried.
After a while they were just another
lump in the snow.

Elwyn was dozing in his chair when there was
a tapping at the window. It was Blitzen. Elwyn
opened the window. Snow flew into the room.
"Say, Elwyn," said Blitzen, "I've been thinking. I'll
bet there are kids who would love to get those toys
of yours."
"Too late now," said Elwyn.
"Don't be so sure," said Blitzen. "Grab that
toboggan and come over to the stable."

When Elwyn got to the stable, the toys
were nowhere to be seen.
Elwyn and Blitzen searched and searched,
but the snow was deep.

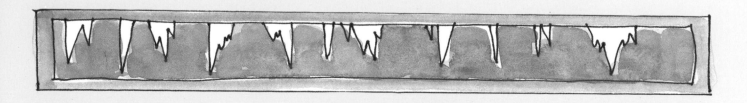

At last they gave up.

"So much for Christmas," said Elwyn.

"At least we tried," said Blitzen. "Hey!
What was that?"

"What was what?" said Elwyn.

"I heard a sound," said Blitzen.
They listened.
Then they both heard the sound,
coming from under a snowdrift.
Cuckoo... Cuckoo...

"The clock!" cried Elwyn. He started
digging in the snow. In a moment
he had found the sack.

"Let's go!" said Blitzen. "It's getting late."

"What do we do?" said Elwyn.

"Get my old harness from that peg at
  the back of the stable," said Blitzen.
"The reins are on the shelf."
"What about these bells?" said Elwyn.
"Want them, too?"
"Might as well do things right," said
  Blitzen. "This will probably be the last
  Christmas ride for both of us."

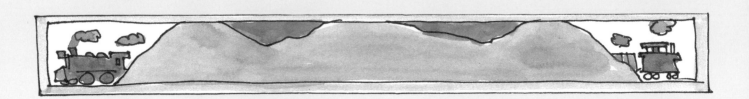

Elwyn climbed onto the toboggan
behind the toys.
"Ready when you are," he said.
"Well, what do you say?" said Blitzen.
"Oh, you mean 'On, Blitzen'?" said
Elwyn.
"That's correct," said Blitzen.
"On, Blitzen!" called Elwyn.

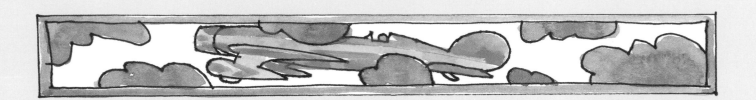

Blitzen broke into a run. The bells
began to jingle. The toboggan went
zigzagging across the snow.
Soon Blitzen's hooves were no longer
touching the snow.
The toboggan swung into the sky.
"Hang on, Elwyn!" called Blitzen.
"We're on our way!"

After a while they saw a city down
below. Santa's sleigh and the
reindeer were standing on a rooftop.
Blitzen landed the toboggan next
to them.

"Look who's here!" said Donner. "It's
 Blitzen!"

"I can't believe it," said Dancer. "How
 did *you* get here?"

"I know the route," said Blitzen.

"And he's *very* fast," said Elwyn.

Just then Santa Claus popped out
of a chimney.
"Well, my goodness," he said. "Blitzen
and Elwyn!"
"We brought some extra toys," said
Elwyn, "if it isn't too late."
"Never too late for toys!" said Santa.
He pointed to the east. "You deliver
in that direction, and we'll deliver
over here!"

He jumped onto his sleigh. "On, Prancer!"
he cried. "On, Dancer! On, Donner
and . . . and . . ."
"Josephine," said Josephine.
"Of course!" said Santa Claus. "On,
 Josephine!"
 Santa's sleigh soared into the sky.
"Ho, ho, ho," he cried.
"On, Blitzen!" said Elwyn. "We haven't
 missed Christmas after all!"
"How about 'ho, ho, ho'?" called Blitzen.
"Ho, ho," said Elwyn.
"Louder!" said Blitzen. "Louder and jollier!"

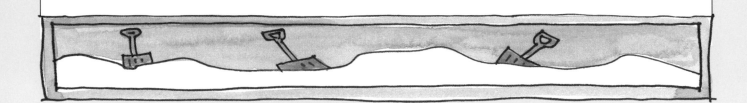

"HO, HO, HO!" cried Elwyn as they galloped
through the night.